REY MYSTERIO:
GIANT SLAYER

BY TRACEY WEST

GROSSET & DUNLAP
Published by the Penguin Group
Penguin Group (USA) Inc., 375 Hudson Street, New York, New York 10014, USA
Penguin Group (Canada), 90 Eglinton Avenue East, Suite 700,
Toronto, Ontario M4P 2Y3, Canada
(a division of Pearson Penguin Canada Inc.)
Penguin Books Ltd., 80 Strand, London WC2R 0RL, England
Penguin Group Ireland, 25 St. Stephen's Green, Dublin 2, Ireland
(a division of Penguin Books Ltd.)
Penguin Group (Australia), 250 Camberwell Road, Camberwell, Victoria 3124, Australia
(a division of Pearson Australia Group Pty. Ltd.)
Penguin Books India Pvt. Ltd., 11 Community Centre, Panchsheel Park,
New Delhi—110 017, India
Penguin Group (NZ), 67 Apollo Drive, Rosedale, Auckland 0632, New Zealand
(a division of Pearson New Zealand Ltd.)
Penguin Books (South Africa) (Pty.) Ltd., 24 Sturdee Avenue,
Rosebank, Johannesburg 2196, South Africa

Penguin Books Ltd., Registered Offices: 80 Strand, London WC2R 0RL, England

ISBN 978-0-448-45708-6   10 9 8 7 6 5 4 3 2

Standing at five feet six inches, Rey Mysterio is shorter than most of the towering Superstars of the WWE. But you won't find him hiding in their shadows. In fact, the man they call Giant Slayer and The Ultimate Underdog has taken down some of the biggest men who've ever stepped inside the ring.

Born in California, Rey Mysterio grew up watching his uncle compete in the high-flying world of *lucha libre*—Mexican wrestling. *Lucha libre* stars are known for wearing colorful masks in the ring. As a teenager, Rey trained in Mexico until he perfected this fast-paced, acrobatic style.

Wrestling fans in the United States loved Rey Mysterio's style. When he came to the WWE in the summer of 2002, the crowd went crazy for him. Rey's first match was against Superstar Chavo Guerrero on *SmackDown*. Chavo came on strong, targeting Rey's ribs and abdomen with powerful kicks and punches.

But Rey turned things around, leaping off the ropes like a bird in flight and slamming into Chavo over and over again. "He's like poetry in motion!" the announcer remarked.

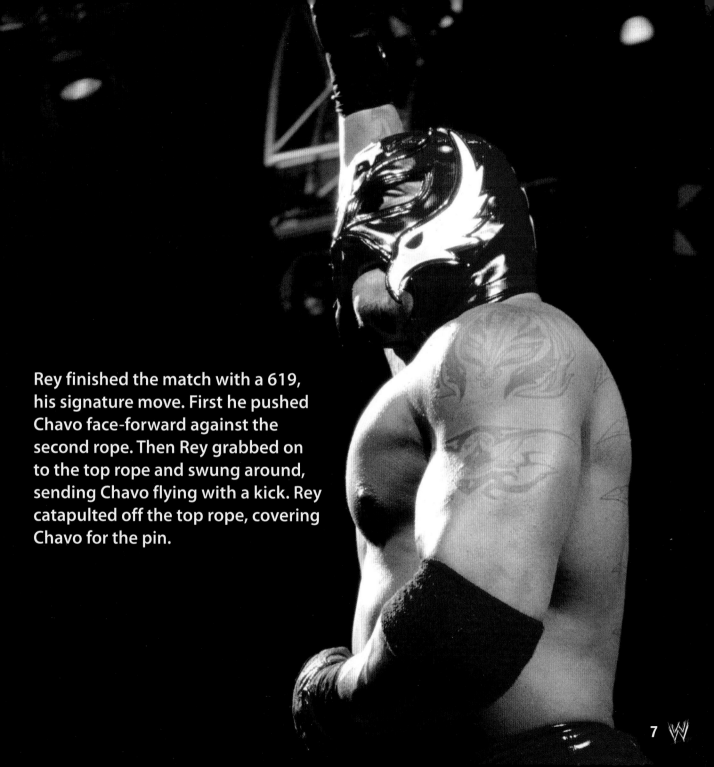

Rey finished the match with a 619, his signature move. First he pushed Chavo face-forward against the second rope. Then Rey grabbed on to the top rope and swung around, sending Chavo flying with a kick. Rey catapulted off the top rope, covering Chavo for the pin.

Rey's WWE career quickly skyrocketed. He formed a tag team with Edge. On November 7, 2002, they faced the current WWE Tag Team Champions in a title match and won. Rey Mysterio had earned his first WWE Championship.

But Rey and Edge didn't hold on to the title for long. Just ten days later, they defended the championship against two other teams at Survivor Series. This time, Chavo Guerrero and his uncle Eddie were also in the ring. It was an intense three-way match, but Los Guerreros became the new WWE Tag Team Champions.

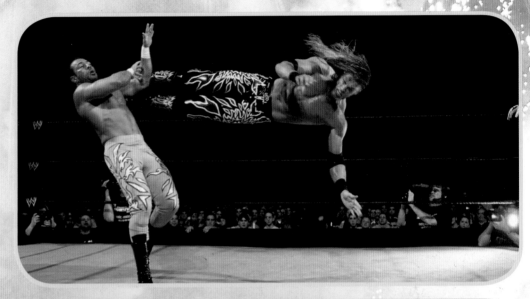

Rey and Edge broke up their tag team after that loss, and Rey set his sights on a new goal: the WWE Cruiserweight Championship. In 2003, that championship belonged to Superstar Matt Hardy. Rey faced off against him at WrestleMania XIX—but Rey lost, partly because Shannon Moore interfered in the match.

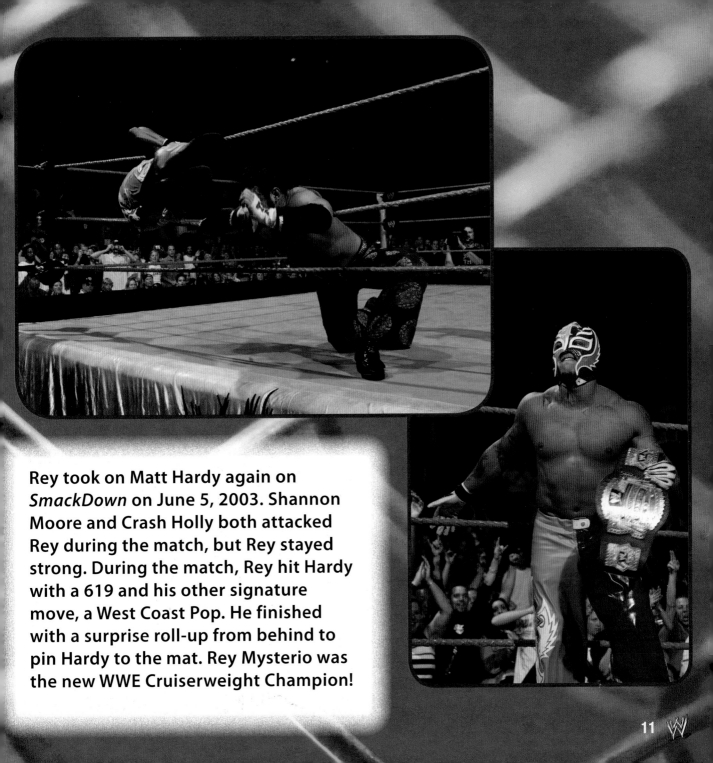

Rey took on Matt Hardy again on *SmackDown* on June 5, 2003. Shannon Moore and Crash Holly both attacked Rey during the match, but Rey stayed strong. During the match, Rey hit Hardy with a 619 and his other signature move, a West Coast Pop. He finished with a surprise roll-up from behind to pin Hardy to the mat. Rey Mysterio was the new WWE Cruiserweight Champion!

Other athletes might have been satisfied taking on opponents their own size—but not Rey. The more skilled he became, the more he wanted the ultimate prize: the WWE World Heavyweight Championship. To do that, Rey would have to take down Superstars nearly twice his size.

At Survivor Series 2005, Rey battled alongside other *SmackDown* Superstars in a fierce brawl against Team *Raw*. Rey found himself in the ring with the Big Red Monster, Kane, and the seven-foot-tall giant, Big Show! Rey's aerial moves helped his team that night, and Team *SmackDown* emerged victorious.

But Rey's biggest moment in the WWE was yet to come. At the Royal Rumble in 2006, he drew the number two slot. That meant he'd have to stay alive in the ring as twenty-eight opponents came in one by one. The odds that Rey would be the last man standing were pretty low.

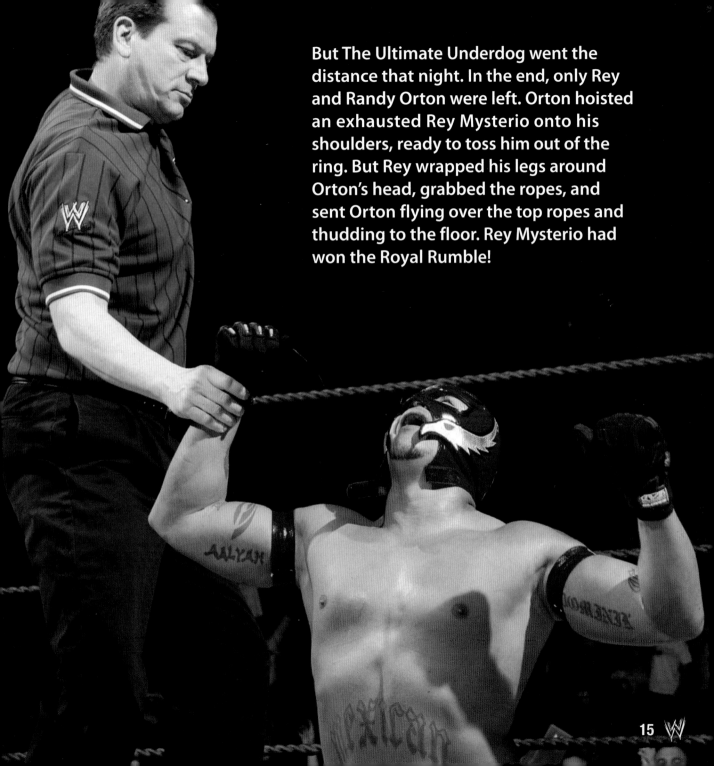

But The Ultimate Underdog went the distance that night. In the end, only Rey and Randy Orton were left. Orton hoisted an exhausted Rey Mysterio onto his shoulders, ready to toss him out of the ring. But Rey wrapped his legs around Orton's head, grabbed the ropes, and sent Orton flying over the top ropes and thudding to the floor. Rey Mysterio had won the Royal Rumble!

Rey's victory earned him the respect of fans around the world—and more. It guaranteed him a shot at the World Heavyweight Championship at the next WrestleMania. But on the next *SmackDown*, Randy Orton taunted Rey, saying he didn't deserve to win. He challenged him to a match at No Way Out. If Rey lost, Orton would get his title shot.

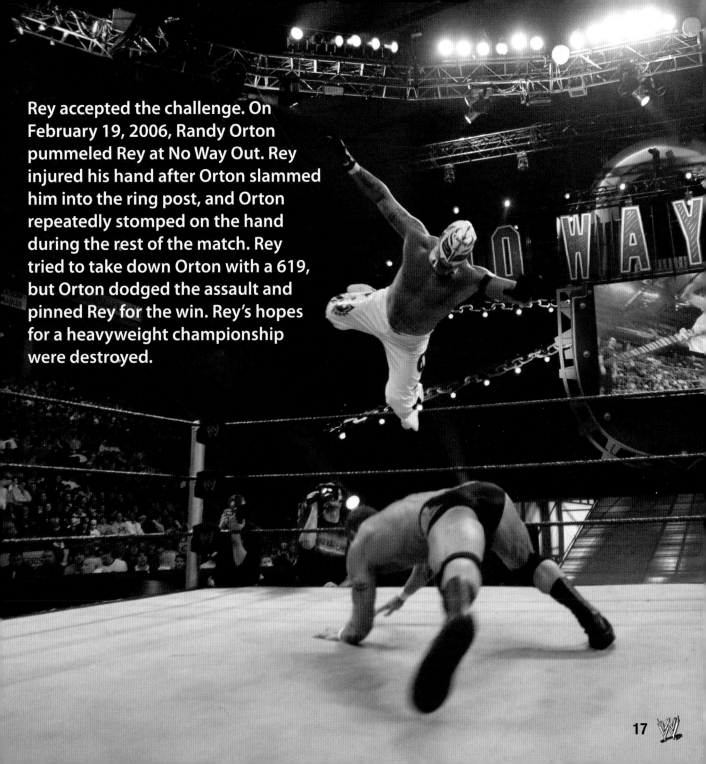

Rey accepted the challenge. On February 19, 2006, Randy Orton pummeled Rey at No Way Out. Rey injured his hand after Orton slammed him into the ring post, and Orton repeatedly stomped on the hand during the rest of the match. Rey tried to take down Orton with a 619, but Orton dodged the assault and pinned Rey for the win. Rey's hopes for a heavyweight championship were destroyed.

Lucky for Rey, *SmackDown* General Manager Theodore Long didn't approve of Orton's illegal moves. He called for a three-way World Heavyweight Championship match at WrestleMania 22—Kurt Angle against Randy Orton and Rey Mysterio.

Kurt Angle dominated the start of the match. He pounded Rey into the mat more than once. Then he got behind Rey so he could perform an Angle Slam, but Rey reversed the move, sending Angle flying out of the ring.

Rey moved quickly, hitting Orton with a 619. Then he finished with a West Coast Pop, jumping off the ropes and swinging his legs around Orton's neck. He covered Orton for the pin to win the World Heavyweight Championship.

"Ladies and gentlemen, dreams do come true!" the announcer cried over the sound of the cheering crowd.

The championship became a target on Rey's back—every Superstar wanted a piece of him now. Nobody wanted it more than John Bradshaw Layfield, known as JBL. The tough Texan and former WWE Champion started a rivalry with Rey.

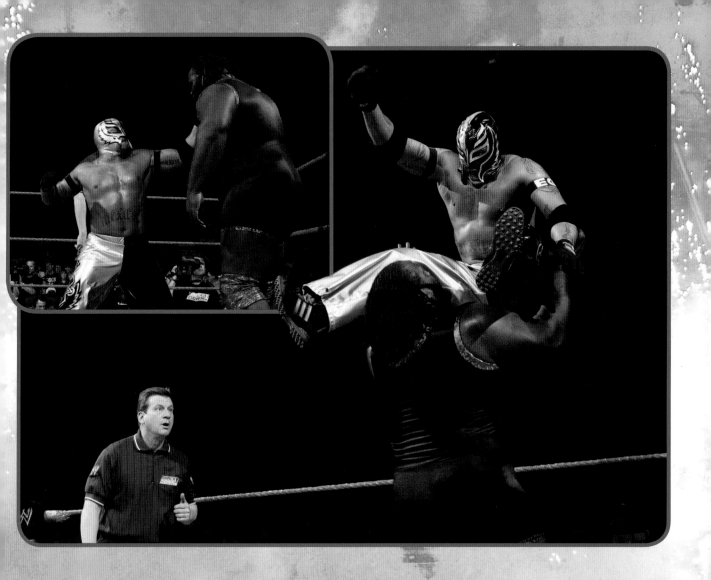

On *SmackDown*, JBL told Rey that he didn't deserve to be a champion. Rey said he'd fight anybody at any time to prove his worth. So JBL set up a match between Rey and The World's Strongest Man, Mark Henry. Rey blasted the big man with a 619, but he couldn't withstand the World's Strongest Slam. Mark Henry won the match—but JBL still wasn't finished with Rey.

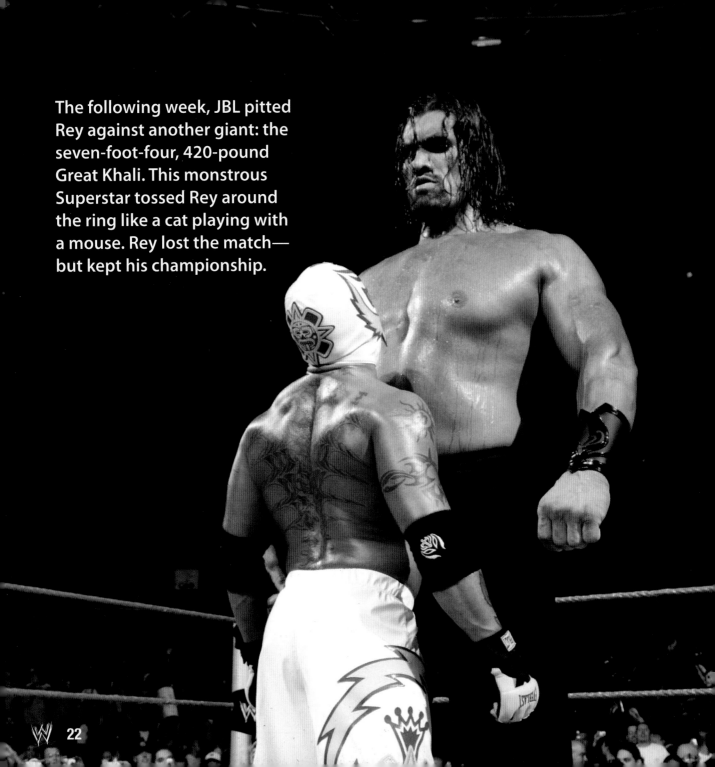

The following week, JBL pitted Rey against another giant: the seven-foot-four, 420-pound Great Khali. This monstrous Superstar tossed Rey around the ring like a cat playing with a mouse. Rey lost the match— but kept his championship.

JBL still wasn't finished testing Rey. One week later, Kane entered the ring with Rey and started pounding the World Heavyweight Champion. The Big Red Monster was acting superstrange that night. After pummeling Rey with a punishing chokeslam, he turned his anger on JBL and chokeslammed him as well. The match ended in a no contest.

Rey bravely faced JBL's challengers one by one. Then, at Judgment Day 2006, the two Superstars faced off in the ring. JBL brought his street-fighting style with him, slapping Rey hard in the face. Rey delivered a 619, but when he tried to finish with a West Coast Pop, JBL threw the ref in the way.

JBL kept up his dirty tricks, but Rey never stooped to his level. When JBL tried to smack him with a folding chair, Rey kicked it into the Texan's face. He followed up with a 619 and a high-flying frog splash that pinned JBL. Rey Mysterio had taken down another giant—and kept his title, too.

Rey would face JBL again in one of the most important matches of his career. At WrestleMania XXV, Rey challenged JBL for the Intercontinental Championship. JBL was still playing dirty—he attacked Rey before the match even started. But once the two Superstars got in the ring, it only took Rey twenty-one seconds to pin JBL.

Now Rey had won four major championships: the Tag Team, Cruiserweight, World Heavyweight, and Intercontinental titles.

These days Rey continues to brawl with the big boys. In 2010 he entered a battle royal. The ring was filled with every *SmackDown* Superstar on the roster. If you were thrown over the top rope and your feet touched the floor, you were out.

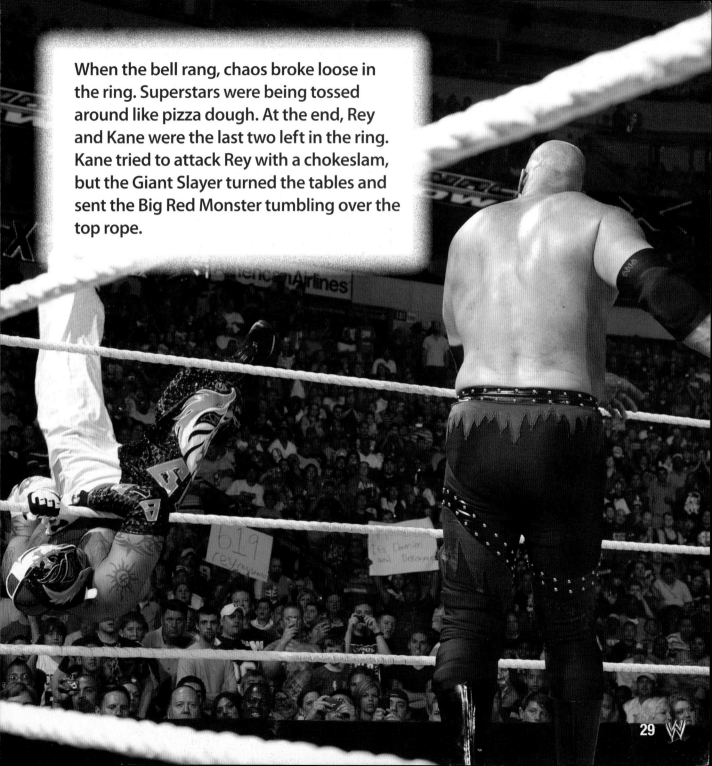

When the bell rang, chaos broke loose in the ring. Superstars were being tossed around like pizza dough. At the end, Rey and Kane were the last two left in the ring. Kane tried to attack Rey with a chokeslam, but the Giant Slayer turned the tables and sent the Big Red Monster tumbling over the top rope.

Rey won a big prize that day: the chance to compete in a World Heavyweight Championship match at the WWE Fatal 4-Way. On June 20, 2010, Rey fought for the title against Jack Swagger, CM Punk, and Big Show.

As usual, Rey was the smallest Superstar in the ring. And, as usual, Rey didn't let that stop him. He allowed the Mysterio magic to take hold: a combination of fearlessness, skill, and agility that's hard to beat. He pinned Jack Swagger to become the World Heavyweight Champion for the second time in his career.

World Heavyweight Champion, Intercontinental Champion, Tag Team Champion, Cruiserweight Champion—there's nothing Rey Mysterio can't do. There may be bigger Superstars in the WWE than him, but Rey's got the heart of a champion—and the titles to prove it.